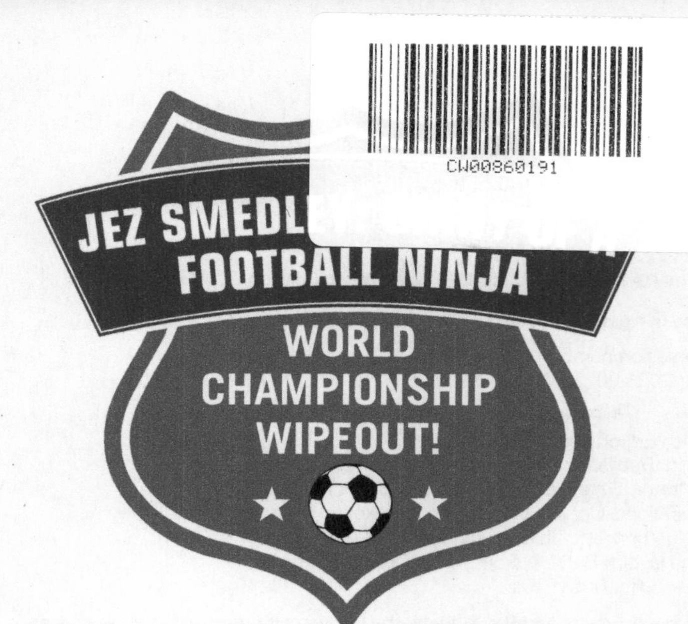

Written by

JEM PACKER

Illustrated by

Gareth Conway

ISBN: 9781510445338

First published in 2019 by Hodder & Stoughton Limited (for its Rising Stars imprint, part of the Hodder Education Group),
An Hachette UK Company
Carmelite House, 50 Victoria Embankment, London EC4Y 0DZ

www.risingstars-uk.com

Impression number 10 9 8 7 6 5 4 3 2 1
Year 2023 2022 2021 2020 2019

Author: Jem Packer
Series Editor: Sasha Morton
Senior Publisher: Helen Parker
Illustrator: Gareth Conway/Bright Group International
Educational Consultant: Catherine Baker
Design concept: Julie Joubinaux
Page layout: Sarah Garbett @ Sg Creative Services
Desk Editor: Amy Tyrer

The publishers would like to thank the following for permission to reproduce copyright material.

Page 22 © lineartestpilot/iStock; page 29 © Can Yesil/Shutterstock; KittyBerriBerri/Shutterstock

With thanks to the schools that took part in the development of *Reading Planet KS2*, including: Ancaster CE Primary School, Ancaster; Downsway Primary School, Reading; Ferry Lane Primary School, London; Foxborough Primary School, Slough; Griffin Park Primary School, Blackburn; St Barnabas CE First & Middle School, Pershore; Tranmoor Primary School, Doncaster; and Wilton CE Primary School, Wilton.

A catalogue record for this title is available from the British Library.

Printed in the United Kingdom

Orders: Please contact Bookpoint Ltd, 130 Park Drive, Milton Park, Abingdon, Oxon OX14 4SE. Telephone: (44) 01235 400555. Email primary@bookpoint.co.uk.

CONTENTS

THE SMEDLEY FAMILY TREE

Grandpa/Grandmaster Sensei Jeffrey Smedley

Mum/Jasmine Smedley

Dad/Josh Smedley

Jez Smedley

Jemima Smedley

Karate-Chomp

THE STORY SO FAR ...

Football-mad friends Jez, Raheem, Big Keith and Viv have formed their very own school football team with Jez's sister, Jemima, in goal – and they are on a winning streak. So far, they have won the Inter-School Cup, the Inter-School National Tournament and, most recently, the European Schools Cup! But, as football ninjas, Jez and the rest of the Smedley family have also confronted a series of super-villains and foiled their cunning plots along the way. Jez and his family have used a series of foot-jitsu moves and a host of footie gadgets to save the day, but this case could be their toughest yet ...

FLYING PHONES!

Now, there are some things in life that just aren't that interesting. Things like doing the washing up, or going to the dentist – you know they're boring, but they just have to be done. Sadly, that day I was doing one of those things, because I was spending Saturday afternoon at … the optician's.

I know we all need to have our eyes tested from time to time but, unfortunately, it always seems to take forever. There's the endless succession of screens to look at and, sorry, but no, Mr Optician, I can't see that letter P that is the size of a full stop. Fortunately, that day I wasn't the one getting their eyes tested.

"Mr Smedley senior," called out the optician, "follow me, please."

Yes, I was accompanying my grandfather, Grandpa Smedley – and whenever he was around, incredible things seemed to happen!

There was the time we went to the zoo and a python escaped. He tracked it down, cornered it by the cafe and wrestled it until its handlers arrived. "Sorry, folks," Grandpa told the cafe's customers. "No burgers or milkshakes until this bad boy is back in his vivarium!"

Then there was the day we went on an excursion to the beach. My ice-cream was attacked by a flock of vicious seagulls, and Grandpa used his kendo skills to fight them off. (Although without a kendo stick, he improvised and fended them off with a cheese baguette!) “Take that you winged brigands!” he shouted as the seagulls made a hasty escape.

Sadly, so far that day all we had done was sit in the optician’s waiting room. I really didn’t know why Grandpa bothered to go since his eyesight was unbelievably good.

“A, E, L, H ...” barked Grandpa as he rapidly read off the top line of letters from the eye chart.

“Can you read the teeny, tiny line at the bottom?” queried the optician.

“O, P, D, Q ...” continued Grandpa.

“Amazing!” cooed the optician. “You have the eyesight of a trained airline pilot one third of your age. Right, try these super-duper tiny letters – I don’t think you have a hope of ever getting these.”

For the first time, Grandpa slowed down, and I could see him squint at the letters.

“I ... J ... That’s a W, yes, W ... and the last one I can’t make out ...”

The optician stopped, and I looked up. So this was it – Grandpa couldn’t read a letter. Was his eyesight finally failing?

“... because a fly has landed on it. It’s flown off now! That’s better. N ...yes, it’s definitely an N,” beamed Grandpa.

“Congratulations, Mr Smedley. You have near-perfect vision!” smiled the optician. “I don’t know how you do it. We’ll see you next year!”

Then something strange happened – something stranger than something super-strange happening on Planet Strange, the strangest planet in the Strange Galaxy. Grandpa decided to buy some glasses anyway!

“I know my eyes are perfect,” he noted. “However, I think glasses make me look debonair, not to mention give me a certain gravitas. I would like to purchase a pair of glasses with clear lenses.”

“Very well, let me order those for you,” declared the slightly confused optician. “I would never get in the way of anyone looking debonair!”

“Excellent,” chuckled Grandpa. We left the optician’s and Grandpa winked at me. “I do believe it’s time for lunch! Let’s eat!”

The great thing about going to the optician's with Grandpa is that, because he has amazing eyesight, the test never lasts very long – and afterwards he treats the whole family to a meal.

"There you are!" Mum had come to meet us. "So, how was it?"

"Oh, Grandpa's eyesight is still as sharp as ever," I said as we made our way to the shopping centre food court. "By the way, where is Jemima?"

I should have guessed. As soon as we arrived at the food court, I spotted her. Well, I didn't so much spot her as spot a teetering pile of textbooks on a table. "Who brings their homework to a restaurant?" I complained.

"I have a very important exam coming up," hissed the pile of books. My sister ALWAYS seemed to have a very important exam coming up.

"You'll have to stop to eat," said Mum.

"Now, where is your father?" asked Grandpa. "I'm hungry. I know, I'll call him."

I should mention that my dad is a hypochondriac. If there is a cold to be caught, he'll catch it; if there is a fever to be gripped by, he'll be gripped by it. He is also accident-prone, so if there is a low ceiling to bump your head on, he'll bump his head on it. So, as I saw Dad approaching, I should have spotted that he was holding his brand-new mobile phone. A phone that Grandpa was now calling, and which was about to ring with a loud, piercing ring that Dad was unaccustomed to hearing … a ring that was about to take him completely by surprise.

“Help! Call an ambulance! My ears! I think they’ve exploded!” screeched Dad as his phone rang.

What happened next seemed to unfold in slow motion as Dad held his head and staggered backwards – towards the staircase that led to the shops below.

I shouted, “STOP!” Too late. Dad was now teetering on the edge of the staircase … one more step back and he would plummet down the stairs.

It was time for some foot-jitsu, so I immediately flew into a lightning leopard turbo dribble round the table and towards Dad, then performed a sliding iron tiger tackle that slid me right behind him and down the stairs. I knew that I would be aching all over the next day, but there was nothing else I could do. I had to become a human trampoline to save my Dad.

KER-RASH!

Dad tumbled down the stairs right on to me. I gasped at the impact. I had saved him! It was then that I noticed something flying straight down towards my head … his new mobile phone! This is it! I thought. I'm about to be knocked unconscious by a mobile phone! Then my sister swung into action. I literally felt the phone graze my head before, at the very last moment, Jemima grabbed it and landed, cat-like, on her feet.

"That was close," smiled Jemima. "Now I've got an appetite!"

The whole restaurant applauded.

"Thanks, guys," huffed Dad. "You know, I've always thought that technology can be dangerous. I'll go and get the drinks …"

"Noooo!" we all cried out in unison.

TECH WEEK

The weekend was soon over and we were back at school. That Monday was also the first day of Technology Week.

"We need more technology in the team," decreed Viv Allvue. She was Throgmorton United's midfield maestro who could pick a pass in the blink of an eye. (In fact, her eyesight was almost as good as Grandpa's.)

"You mean a computer programme to track our movements," mused Raheem. "I'm sorry, but they haven't invented a processor that's able to keep up with me!" Raheem Blast was our striker, renowned for his hammer-like shot and incredible speed.

"Hi-tech and me don't really mix," grumbled Big Keith, our concrete-shinned defender. "I tend to break most machines I come across."

"I'm all for it," I said boldly. "Anything that could gain us an advantage has to be worth looking at."

Usually, at this time of the morning Mr Drabble would sound the school bell, but today, instead of hearing the traditional ringing noise, we heard a loud, high-pitched warble. This noise finally gave way to an even louder sound:

"GOOD MORNING, EVERYBODY!" boomed our super-enthusiastic form teacher, Mrs Norbertson. "How do you like the new, electronic school bell? Jez?"

"It's very ... er ... hi-tech," I mumbled, my ears still humming from the high-pitched cacophony.

"Exactly! It's Technology Week, and it's time to modernise our school," continued Mrs Norbertson. "For our latest class project, I want you to think about technology, specifically wearable technology. Raheem, can you give an example of wearable technology?"

It was over to Raheem to come up with a quick answer, and I could see he was struggling.

"Er, yes, wearable, er, let me see, wearable technology," he stuttered. I don't think any of us had ever seen Raheem be this slow! "A hat made from, er, from waterproof material ..."

"That might have been considered wearable technology fifty years ago," smiled Mrs Norbertson. "I want something more hi-tech than that. What about you, Keith?"

Poor Keith was on the spot, but as he wracked his brains the classroom door burst open. It was our head teacher, Mr Drabble, and he seemed to be in a full-blown panic.

"Close the class computer down right away!" barked our frantic head teacher. Mrs Norbertson could tell by his tone of voice that this was not a joke, and she quickly shut the computer down.

"What's going on?" she asked.

"There has been a vicious cyber attack on the school's computer system!" he announced. "The school dinner order of burgers and ice-cream has been changed to turnips and Brussels sprouts."

We all groaned – school lunches were about to get even worse.

"There's more," continued Mr Drabble. "The school order of loo rolls has been sent to my home address, and we seem to have two hundred extra cleaners booked for next Sunday. I have no idea what will happen next!"

It didn't take long for us to find out because, suddenly, the class computer switched itself back on!

"What's happening?" cried Mrs Norbertson. "This thing has a mind of its own!"

"We need urgent IT support!" wailed Mr Drabble.

"Let me have a look," said Viv, who was the class computer expert. She started tapping away on the keyboard. "Yes, it's definitely a cyber attack and … wait! There's a message coming through!"

The computer now started to talk, and a harsh, barking voice could be heard through the system's speaker!

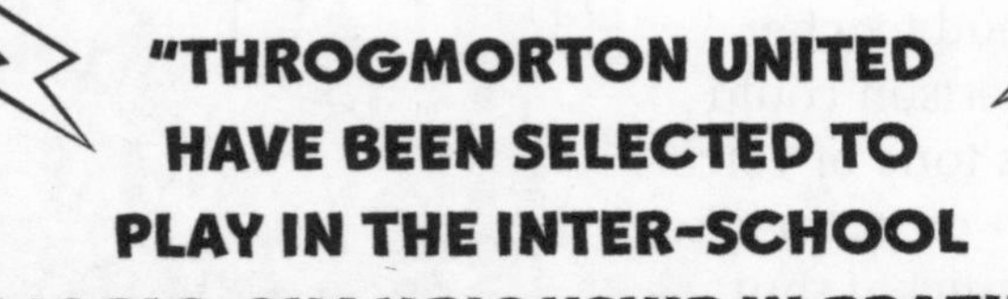

“Hey, that’s great news!” said Mr Drabble. “The best teams from all over the world will gather to play for a prestigious international trophy – a shield bearing all the flags of the world. There were a number of complicated forms …”

But we were so excited we had already drowned out our head teacher’s monologue.

“Fantastic!” I shouted.

“Yippee!” boomed Raheem.

“Hurray!” bellowed Big Keith.

Viv was now urgently tapping on the computer keyboard. There was a loud fizz and an oddly electronic bang before the computer closed down normally.

“I think I’ve deleted the virus.” said Viv calmly.

“We all need an early break,” smiled Mr Drabble, delighted that the school computers seemed to be back to normal, for now. “I’m sure Mrs Norbertson won’t mind, just this once?”

"Don't forget the project, class!" said Mrs Norbertson as we filed out of the classroom. "I want you to invent your own creative and innovative item of wearable technology. However, if your computer at home shows any signs of playing up, call Viv!"

"Although Viv will now be spending much of her time, along with her teammates, training for their trip to Brazil," said Mr Drabble – as if we needed any reminding.

In the playground, we soon formed a huddle as we had a lot to discuss!

"So, we need to arrange extra training sessions," I said. "I'll speak to Mr Drabble about booking the school pitch."

"We need to pack our bags for Brazil," piped up Raheem. "Fast!" He was always in a great hurry – a bit like the way he played football!

"Slow down, Raheem," said Big Keith. "We have to get our play up to its highest standard yet before we even think about the trip."

"Oh yes, and we also need to work on the Technology Week project," warned Viv. "I think I have the perfect idea that will cover both football and wearable technology …"

There was just so much to think about and, as I walked home after school later that day, I had no doubt that this was going to be our biggest challenge yet. As we planned our next training session, little did I know that across town something malevolent was unfolding.

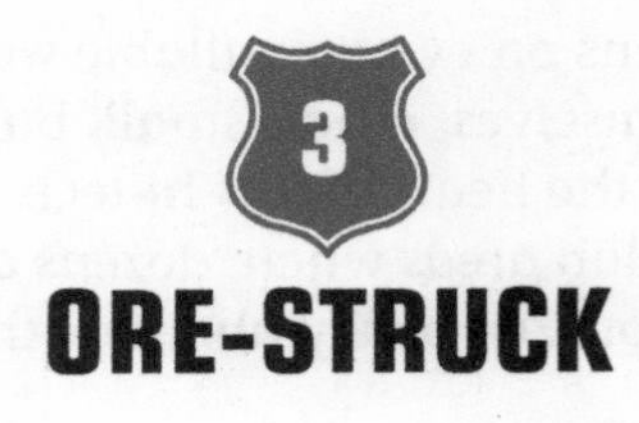

ORE-STRUCK

A short, stout man with a mop of curly hair and a brightly coloured Hawaiian shirt swaggered into Hi-Tech Toys International: a shop that, as its name suggested, specialised in hi-tech toys. If you were looking for a remote-controlled car, an ultra-advanced drone or the latest video games, Hi-Tech Toys was the place to go. The swaggering man was Darren Bad-Pixel, and the toyshop belonged to him.

"Good evening," grinned Bad-Pixel, addressing the woman behind the counter. Then, checking the shop was empty, he continued, "I think it's time to close the store."

"Of course," replied the woman. Her red hair was tied back in a tight ponytail. She had sharp cheekbones and was wearing a white lab coat. Her name was Lavinia Tech, and – like the shop – there was more to her than met the eye. As she pressed a couple of buttons behind the counter, the shutters closed on the shopfront, the till calculated the day's takings and, most significantly, a section of the shop floor began to move. This section slid smoothly aside to reveal an opening to a staircase below.

"To the lair," cackled Bad-Pixel as they walked down the dimly lit staircase.

Although the toyshop was of average size and the staircase was small and narrow, nothing could prepare anyone for what lay at the foot of those stairs. Here, a vast cavern extended as far as the eye could see.

There were screens on every available wall – some as big as the walls themselves, others small, but all buzzing with activity. At the heart of this hi-tech complex was a series of huge lab areas where dozens of workers in white lab coats buzzed busily about as they worked on experiments.

"Join me in my pod, Lavinia," said Bad-Pixel with a sly grin. A drone pod about the size of a small garden shed with a glass dome and two seats buzzed down from the high ceiling. This was Bad-Pixel's mobile office, and it enabled him to zip around from area to area inside the huge lair to monitor his inventors, who were working silently on computers, and observe his research scientists, who were scrutinising bubbling vats and tinkering with experimental machines.

"My plan is almost complete," he said, smiling unpleasantly to his wicked sidekick. "Come with me and let me bring you up to speed."

The drone pod zipped silently around the colossal cavern as Bad-Pixel described his plan to his most senior accomplice.

"As you know, scientists at my top-secret laboratory have been working around the clock," began Bad-Pixel as they zoomed over to the largest bank of computers.

"And as you instructed, I recruited the finest evil minds from around the world," interrupted Lavinia.

"Indeed you did, and they have done a terrific job," continued Bad-Pixel in a reassuring tone. "I can now hack and control almost any computer, smartphone or tablet device in the world at will. But ..."

The drone pod now swooped down to a new area where computer devices, mobile phones and tablets were being manufactured on a slick production line.

"I've decided to turn the plan on its head," said Bad-Pixel. "Even the best hacks can be countered ..."

“There are lots of computer experts out there,’ nodded Lavinia. “Not to mention super-smart school kids.”

“So, rather than try to hack computers and handheld devices, why not make the devices themselves? If I make the machines, I can access them when I like and how I like.”

“Bank details, personal ID all on tap for you to access whenever you want,” whispered an awestruck Lavinia. “That is most impressive – but aren’t there lots of companies who make electronic devices already? Why would people choose to purchase your devices?”

“Simple. Because my machines will be half the price of everyone else’s,” said Bad-Pixel. “Take a closer look at this development area. I’ve devised a way of making electronics ultra-cheaply.”

The drone pod was now at ground level, gliding alongside the laboratory’s mass production line. Here, mobile phones and tablet devices were being assembled at an impressive rate.

“This is fantastic!” said Lavinia. “At this rate, we’ll get one of your devices in every hand in the world in no time.”

But when Lavinia looked over at her boss, she realised Bad-Pixel had stopped smiling. His face had darkened with anger.

“There’s one teeny, weeny problem,” complained Bad-Pixel. “The material that allows me to make these machines so cheaply is called phonium. It’s an ore, and only I know how to use it to make computer chips.”

“So, we buy all the phonium in the world,” shrugged Lavinia.

"That's the trouble," sighed Bad-Pixel. "It's not for sale. We will have to mine it ourselves and, of course, I don't want anyone else knowing what I'm doing."

"So, where's this phonium located?" enquired Lavinia. "We'll buy the land, we'll evict anyone who lives there, we'll chop down the forests, drain the lakes – do whatever it takes ..."

"It's not as simple as that," said Bad-Pixel as he pressed a button and a huge, virtual screen crackled into view in front of them. "The phonium is located on the other side of the world in a built-up area. The main concentration is in one specific place, in one specific country."

"Brazil?" said Lavinia as the drone pod hovered in front of the area of the map that was glowing red.

"Yes, and ninety-five per cent of the world's phonium supply is in one particular city in Brazil," stated Bad-Pixel. "It's time for a carnival of nastiness, my dear. We're going to Rio de Janeiro!"

STEEL OX

I found that the weeks after the Brazil trip announcement flew by in a bit of a blur of football training and experiments in football technology.

Mrs Norbertson had produced a guide to our school project …

SCHOOL TECHNOLOGY WEEK CONTINUES!

PROJECT:

You must find a novel form of wearable technology – the more unexpected the better!

Either demonstrate an original way of wearing existing technology or invent your own!

GOOD LUCK!

My attempt at wearable technology – perma-stick goalie gloves (gloves that automatically held on to the ball) – had gone horribly wrong. The gloves ended up permanently stuck to the fridge door. Then my pet hamster, Karate-Chomp, fell in a failed batch of the glue and became temporarily affixed to my bedroom ceiling. It took three hours to get him down!

Raheem had tried to construct a remote-controlled boot that enabled perfect ball control on pressing a button, but the electronics in the controller had got so overheated that it had melted his sports bag.

Big Keith attempted to create electronic socks that used a computer programme to calculate the optimum moment to shoot. Alarmingly, they had malfunctioned the first time he tried them on and he had kicked the school bus, leading to a sprained big toe.

Finally, Viv kept promising that she was about to deliver the perfect gadget but it was still 'in development'.

Despite all the team football sessions and gadget-developing, one thing never stopped – when the gong sounded in the Smedley household, it meant only one thing – that it was time for **NINJA TRAINING!**

That day, when the gong rang out, I dashed to the kitchen where the concealed entrance to our secret dojo was located. Mum pushed the granola jar on the fridge, revealing the entrance to a lift. We hopped in and were soon descending into the basement below our house.

There to meet us was Grandpa, or Grandmaster Smedley as he was also known, the head of foot-jitsu training – although he looked a little different.

"Greetings, Team Smedley – time to train!"

"Er, Grandmaster," said Dad gingerly. "I can't help but notice ..."

"The glasses?" interrupted Grandmaster Smedley. "Don't need them, as Jez knows, but I thought they made me look, I don't know, sophisticated and refined."

"Refined?" chuckled Dad. "But you're a martial arts expert. Why would you want to look 'refined'?"

Grandpa shot Dad a look that sent him nervously trotting off to mission control for his own safety.

“I have some software to fine tune,” Dad muttered as he hurried away.

“Well, I think those glasses suit you. In fact, they make you look intellectual and dapper, so there!” piped up Mum, trying to save the situation. “Now, I have some gadgets to work on.”

That cleared the air and, with a sigh of relief, Jemima and I got down to work. Our usual routine was that I worked on foot-jitsu moves in the dojo with my sister, while my parents worked in their own areas: Dad in mission control and Mum in her gadget gallery. That day, unusually – and because of the school project – I requested a change of plan.

"Mum, can I work with you today?" I wheedled. Mum, who as well as being a sports master is also a rocket scientist (yes, an actual rocket scientist) and brilliant at making football-related gadgets, didn't look impressed.

"Jez, I am aware of your school project," frowned Mum. "You know there is no way I can allow you to take any of my top-secret ninja gadgets to school – although I am working on something really exciting."

"Project Shin Pad?" I enquired. "The perfect wearable technology!" Mum had mentioned this ongoing project to me in passing, but had sworn me to secrecy.

"Oh yes," grinned Mum. "Don't worry, you'll view my futuristic shin pads soon enough."

I was excited to see Mum's latest gadget, but disappointed not to be able to take it to school. I knew her hi-tech shin pads would have gone down a storm with Mrs Norbertson. Not only that but, unlike my sticky gloves, Mum's gadgets actually worked!

"That's quite enough chatter about gadgets," growled Grandmaster Smedley. "The young Smedleys have training to do! Today, we will be revising the three primary skills. Jez, iron tiger tackle!"

I flew through the air and crashed into my sister in a bid to get the ball. Well, that's what I tried to do but, as I was about to make contact with her, she flicked the ball away and dribbled off with it at her feet!

"Nice lightning leopard turbo dribble! I taught you well, Jemima. That move was next on my list," smiled Grandmaster Smedley.

Meanwhile, I was still struggling to pick myself off the ground, where I lay in a crumpled heap.

"Come on, Jez. That was almost a great tackle. Unfortunately, you tried it on a fellow football ninja," said Grandmaster Smedley. "Okay, Jemima, lob the ball to Jez."

My sister picked the ball up and threw it high into the air. As it plummeted back towards the dojo floor, Grandpa roared, **"FLYING DRAGON HEADER!"**

I now sprang high in the air and, using every muscle in my neck, headed the ball with such power it became a blur – a blur that was heading straight towards Grandmaster Smedley and his sparkling new glasses! Once a football ninja, always a football ninja – Grandpa jumped into the air and kicked the ball back at me with such force that, for the second time, I found myself flat on my back!

"That was impressive! Was that the legendary steel ox super shot?" asked Jemima as she helped me back to my feet. "I've read about it in the foot-jitsu history books."

"Yes, and you are about to be instructed in how to do it. It's a shot that can literally burst through the back of the net. I used it to best effect many years ago in the case of the Purple Polar Bear," continued Grandpa. "I cornered him in a jeweller's in Karachi and knocked him into the store's vault with the steel ox super shot."

But then he remembered why we were there. "Right, then. Reminiscing is all very well, but it's back to training for you two!"

As we got to work on our new move, Mum and Dad appeared with some worrying news.

"We've detected a spike in computer-hacking activity all over town," announced Dad. "We're trying to pinpoint the source, but the hackers have covered their tracks really well."

"I think we may be dealing with some kind of computer-whizz super-villain," warned Mum. "Every football ninja needs to be on a high state of alert as we try to work out who's doing this, and why!"

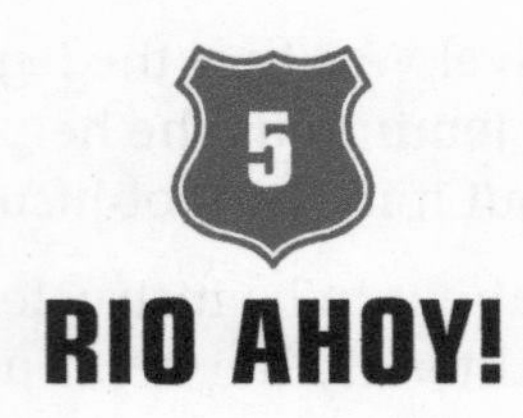

RIO AHOY!

For the next few days, we stepped up our training and took it to a new level of intensity. Not only did Grandmaster Smedley run our foot-jitsu drills endlessly, but Mum and Dad worked round the clock on gadgets and mission planning. It was a frustrating time for all the family: Jemima and I were finding the new move hard to master, and my parents still had no idea about the source of the computer hacking.

"Football training today!" said Jemima. In all the excitement of a new case, we had almost forgotten about the international tournament.

"Last session before we make the trip!" smiled Mum as we came off the pitch. Although work in the dojo was tough and frustrating, on the training field Throgmorton United had never looked so good.

"We've got new formations, new moves, new set-piece routines," I declared. "Bring on Brazil!"

***

At the airport the next day, everyone was super-excited to be heading to South America. As we waited for our flight in the departure lounge, we were all soon gathered around Raheem's tablet.

"I've got a great travel app that tells us all about Brazil," he said, and we were soon poring over lots of amazing facts about Brazil.

Brazil is renowned for its love of football, a passion that has brought it huge success in international tournaments.

Brazil is famous for its diverse and spectacular wildlife, much of it located in the Amazon, the largest rainforest in the world.

As well as boasting a plethora of wildlife, Brazil is also noted for its spectacular cities: from Rio de Janeiro, famed for its beaches and carnival, to São Paulo, the largest city.

Brazil has an extraordinary Atlantic coastline that totals 7491 kilometres. There are also numerous islands and the second longest river in the world, the Amazon.

The official language of Brazil is Portuguese. This makes it unique among Latin American countries, the rest of whom have Spanish as their first language.

"This information is amazing," I said with a smile, but no sooner had I uttered these words than the tablet started to splutter and fizz!

"What's going on?" said Raheem. "This device is brand new!"

"I think you should switch it off," warned Viv as smoke started to emerge from the side of the tablet.

“That’s strange,” I mused, my ninja senses tingling. “Brand-new tablets don’t just break down for no reason.”

“Jez, Jemima, why don’t you stretch your legs?” suggested Mum. “I think you need to have a snoop around.” Mum winked at me as she realised what had happened to the hand-held computer.

While the rest of the team tucked into their packed lunches, Jemima and I slipped off. We explored the airport, not knowing exactly what we were looking for. Despite perusing every corner, we hadn’t detected anything suspicious.

In the food court, the usual mix of tourists and business travellers were eating and drinking in the usual mix of restaurants and cafes. Some would occasionally glance up at the announcement board; others were reading newspapers and books. It was then that we noticed that all those using laptops and mobile devices seemed to be having problems.

"There seems to be an airport-wide issue," I whispered. "But why?"

We immediately concentrated our surveillance on anyone using electronic equipment. It was only then that I realised how futile that was.

"Almost everyone is on a device, Jemima," I sighed, deciding to return to the rest of the team. "We should warn Mum and Dad that something weird is happening across the airport."

On our way back, we once again passed through the shopping area with its typical selection of perfume and sunglasses stores. Then I spotted it: Electronic Paradise.

A shop selling electronic devices wasn't surprising in itself, but what was happening at the back was. Here, a man in a vividly coloured shirt, standing next to a woman in a white lab coat, was frantically typing on a display laptop. It wasn't the kind of typing you would associate with a browsing shopper, and – even more strangely – there was no sign of a shop assistant.

"Excuse me!" I said, but no sooner had I spoken than they scarpered, quickly slipping through the 'Staff only' door. Jemima and I took a closer look to discover something even more peculiar – this door required an electronic badge to open it, and the departing duo certainly didn't look like staff. Any chance to investigate further disappeared as we were interrupted by an announcement.

"FLIGHT 2364 TO RIO DE JANEIRO, BRAZIL, IS DEPARTING FROM GATE 14.

REPEAT: FLIGHT 2364 TO RIO DE JANEIRO, BRAZIL, IS DEPARTING FROM GATE 14."

As soon as we boarded the plane, I told Mum and Dad all about our strange encounter in the shop.

"I noticed my laptop was behaving oddly," said Dad, before running off to the toilet.

"Air sickness," sighed Mum.

"We haven't even taken off yet," I muttered as Dad was escorted back to his seat by a flight attendant.

"Just the thought of flying is making me queasy," complained Dad, whose face had drained of all colour.

Fortunately, the rest of the long flight passed without incident. We got some sleep, Mum gave us a detailed talk about tactics and we looked out at the ocean below. After a second meal and a film, the shimmering lights of the city were eventually twinkling beneath us. As soon as we touched down, I forgot all about odd characters and malfunctioning tablets. We were in Rio de Janeiro!

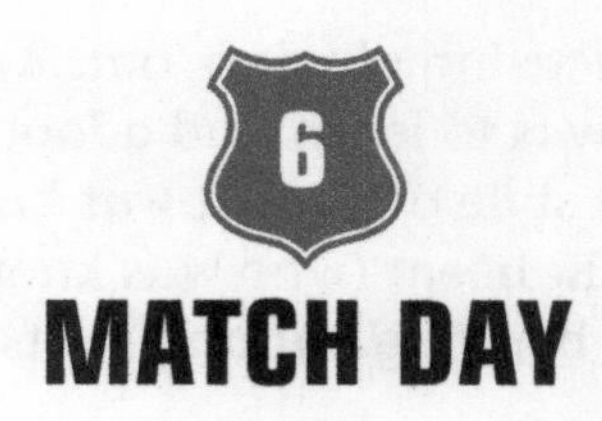

MATCH DAY

Luckily, we had a couple of days to acclimatise to the heat – the weather in Rio was like nothing any of us had encountered before.

"Super-hot and mega-humid," gasped Mr Drabble who, for some reason, insisted on wearing his suit and tie; the rest of us were in shorts and T-shirts. Dad, who was allergic to the heat, refused to leave the air-conditioned hotel room where he spent his time in an ice-cold bath, having the occasional cold shower and ordering regular ice-creams from room service.

The rest of us, though, were having a great time, which only got better when Mum announced that our training was going to take place on a pitch in a rather amazing location.

"Copacabana Beach!" she declared as we reached the glorious expanse of shimmering sand and crystal-clear water. "But no swimming until training is completed."

For the next couple of days, we settled into our surroundings and into a new routine. We would walk from the hotel to the training pitch across the street, where Mum had us working on new tactics and routines for our forthcoming games.

Mum and Mr Drabble had devised a brand-new strategy, which they hoped would give us a chance against some of the teams we would be playing against.

We were now practising playing 'outside our comfort zones'. The idea was to learn and adopt new elements into our personal style of play. It was hard work, but wonderful to see Raheem (who was known for his power kick) working on bending banana shots.

"Come on!" yelled Mum. "You've got to really wrap your foot around it."

Jemima was practising trying to save these bending banana shots, which was really challenging as they would twist and turn at the last moment. Viv, who was great at long passes, was now being coached to practise short, quick passes. As for me, well I got to practise all of these!

One player, however, was finding this particularly hard: Big Keith. As the team's tough-tackling, no-nonsense defender, he had to work on his pace, skill and dribbling.

This was NOT his speciality, but – as Mum said – it might make the difference between winning and losing. Although Big Keith was finding it gruelling, we all admired his work ethic as he did his best to charge up and down the pitch as quickly as he could.

"Great job, Keith," beamed Mr Drabble. "You seem to have found second gear – let's aim for third before our big game tomorrow!"

As the final practice session ended, Viv announced she had something to show us. "Remember Mrs Norbertson's project?" she asked.

"We're in Brazil, Viv. I thought only Jemima thought about school over here!" joked Raheem.

"Well, I've been working on a gadget and I think now is the time to try it," continued Viv. "I call it 'the footie headband'. It has an in-built processor to measure your dribbling speed, tackle strength and shooting accuracy."

"Mrs Norbertson requested a creative item of wearable technology – and it's the first football-specific headband I've ever seen," said Raheem, impressed at this bit of kit. "I hope it can keep up with me!"

"They'll transmit the data to Jez's dad for analysis on his laptop," continued Viv. "They're prototypes, so I hope they work. Oh yes, and I have checked with the tournament organisers – we are allowed to wear them."

The next morning, we were all wearing our footie headbands as we took a coach to the football stadium. We were nervous and excited to finally be playing our first match.

"As long as I have a constant supply of ice cubes, I'll be fine," groaned Dad, who was emerging from the hotel into the blazing sunshine for the first time. "I've got a heat rash the size of the Amazon rainforest on my chest."

"Too much information!" snapped Mum as we arrived at the stadium. In the very centre of the city, the stadium was hemmed in by tall skyscrapers on all four sides. As we entered the arena and examined the pitch, what really struck us was the colour of the ground. A strange, reddy-coloured earth was visible between the sparse patches of grass.

"There's hardly any grass on it," noted Big Keith. "I suppose it's because it's so hot here."

We didn't have long to examine the pitch as our opponents were already out, warmed up and waiting for us. Our first game was against South Africa FC, and it was clear right from the outset that this was going to be a tough assignment! No sooner had the whistle blown than their players were making powerful runs all over the pitch, challenging us hard for every ball and generally playing a high-octane brand of football.

"We knew these would be our hardest games ever," I gasped as Jemima picked the ball out of the back of the net. "This team are world class!"

0-1

Something odd happened as we played: each of us felt an unfamiliar buzz on our heads from the footie headbands. They were evaluating our performances, and I could see Dad furiously typing away at his laptop on the sidelines. We all lifted our levels and, although we created very few chances, we were able to hang on until half-time. As we

trooped off the pitch, we were expecting Mum to address us but, unusually, it was Dad who spoke first.

“I’ve been going through the data from your footie headbands and can tell you each where you need to improve.” He then proceeded to give us each an individual breakdown of our numbers, including scores for effort, percentage of shots missed, number of tackles made.

“This is far too complicated,” complained Big Keith. “Apparently, my ‘tackle percentage’ is fifty-three per cent. What does that mean?”

"Don't worry," interrupted Mum. "I'll explain. Jez, you need to increase the amount of ground you are covering. Raheem, you need to attempt three times more shots. Viv, pass quicker, and Keith, you are going in for the tackle too early. Oh, and last but not least, Jemima, you need to find a teammate with your goal kicks more often."

It was an unusual team talk, but given the current score and the standard of the opposition, we were willing to try anything. The second half kicked off and, with Mum's words still ringing in our ears, we were soon working hard to get back into the match.

I ran my socks off attempting to cover every blade of grass (or, rather, every square inch of red soil). Viv passed in a blur of short, sharp pinpoint passes, mostly fed by Jemima's accurately passed clearances, and Big Keith tackled beautifully. It was now down to Raheem and what he could do up front. So – as Mum had told him – he now adopted a 'shoot on sight' policy. And it paid off. After a quick passing interchange with first Viv, then me, he powered a great shot past the South African keeper.

1-1!

We then hung on as they attacked our goal mercilessly. Somehow, we made it to the final minute – when I fed the ball to Raheem who curled a peach (or should that be banana?) of a shot into the top corner.

2-1!

"Great work!" cried Mr Drabble as we shook hands with our opponents and left the pitch, tired but elated. "Great play backed up by a little hi-tech won the day!"

PROBLEMO

The joy from our match success was short-lived because, as we set off back to the hotel, it soon became apparent that something was wrong.

"I thought this trip was meant to take twenty minutes," wailed Dad "I'm burning up in here."

"It seems the driver's sat nav isn't working properly," said Mr Drabble. "Good thing I have an old-fashioned map. I'll direct him back to the hotel."

Mr Drabble's directions worked, eventually, but when we got to the hotel the problems only got worse.

"I'm sorry, but there is an issue with the electronic room keys," the receptionist explained apologetically. "We hope to be able to open your rooms soon."

As my parents checked their malfunctioning phones, my sister was unable to do her homework on her laptop and Raheem's tablet stopped working once again. It became clear that the whole city was under some sort of cyber attack! When we finally made it to our rooms, Mum and Dad didn't take long to swing into action.

"I'm making a mission control in the bathroom," declared Dad. "It won't hurt to be close to a cold shower."

"I'll make a mini gadget gallery on the balcony," said Mum.

"Who'll take training?" I asked.

"Dad can't leave the hotel unless he's on an air-conditioned bus," added Jemima.

Just then, there was a knock at the door and a familiar-looking figure appeared.

"Grandpa!" I cried.

"As soon as I found out what was happening here, I decided I had to join you. I'll be taking training bright and early tomorrow morning!" he declared.

***

On the other side of Rio, something sinister was happening at a branch of Hi-Tech Toys International.

"This is the perfect place to carry out my plan," purred Bad-Pixel as he surveyed his new surroundings. "I think all international villains should have their own worldwide chain of shops. It makes overseas villain work so much easier."

"It's perfect, sir," said Lavinia, furiously fanning herself. "Just like our home base, but hotter."

"Everything is in place for world domination," exclaimed Bad-Pixel. "I can now control most phones and laptops at will. Didn't we have fun at the airport!?"

"Brilliant, and you can stop all sat navs at the press of a button," added Lavinia. "Not to mention electronic hotel keys."

"Just wait until EVERY device in the world is made by me," chortled Bad-Pixel. "All I need for the next phase of the plan is phonium – lots and lots of it."

"About that … I have drones surveying the whole city, and they have uncovered vast quantities of the stuff. There's one itsy-bitsy, teeny-weeny problemo," sighed

Lavinia quietly.

"I don't like it when you say 'problemo'," snarled Bad-Pixel. "It normally means an enormous, colossal, vast problem with sprinkles on top."

"Well, you could say that," murmured Lavinia. She pressed a button, and a large screen crackled into view. On the screen was a picture of downtown Rio, complete with tower blocks, roads and pavements.

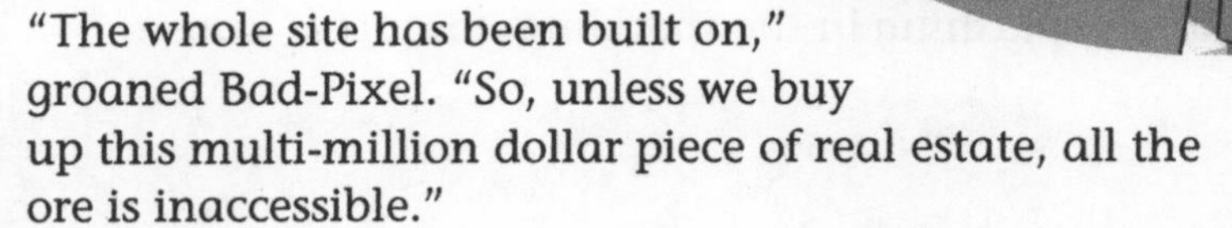

"The whole site has been built on," groaned Bad-Pixel. "So, unless we buy up this multi-million dollar piece of real estate, all the ore is inaccessible."

"Not quite all," smiled Lavinia. "The drones are trying to find any areas that haven't been built on. All we need is a small area to start our excavation and we could still extract the amount we need. We may take a building or two down in the process, but that won't stop us."

"Well, get a move on " snapped Bad-Pixel. "World domination awaits!"

OUTDOOR DOJO

The next day, as Mum and Dad remained in the hotel to work on gadgets and mission planning, Jemima and I hit the beach – but this wasn't a bathing expedition!

"Right, behold the beach dojo," beamed Grandpa proudly that morning. "I have recreated our home dojo by the sea, but I don't want anyone getting distracted by ice-creams, and don't even think about snorkelling."

You had to hand it to Grandpa – he had only been in Rio for a short while, but he had already created an al fresco dojo, complete with coconuts for plastic cones, a driftwood goal and an assault course made from palm leaves and deckchairs.

"It's so tempting," I groaned as I enviously looked at bathers splashing in the sparkling, turquoise waters.

"Okay, maybe a quick dip after training," said Grandpa, who was a bit of a surfer on the side. "But first – chase!"

Grandpa threw a ball high into the air, and Jemima and I dashed across the sand.

"This is going to be the toughest training ever," warned Grandmaster Smedley, who seemed to be relishing the heat. "Time for foot-jitsu!"

We practised our steel ox super shot for the next hour, smashing the ball from one side of the beach to the other. It was hot, exhausting work, but there was no doubt my shot was getting stronger.

"The key is to concentrate your inner energy, focus on the ball, then … like a coiled spring … unleash!" said Grandmaster Smedley. "You must be like the ox that has spotted some tasty grass on the other side of a fence. Then, like the hungry ox, put all your force into forward momentum."

"Like this?" I asked, unleashing an almighty shot that almost knocked Jemima over.

"No, like this," Grandmaster Smedley corrected me. He then hit the ball so hard that it turned into a blur. Jemima wisely withdrew her hand from trying to stop it at the last second.

"I need to have all my fingers for the next match," she noted.

***

We were soon on the coach and heading back to the stadium. Mum was drilling us on the tactics for the next game, but Grandpa was distracted.

"Look at the sky," he warned as we approached the stadium.

"Drones," whispered Mum. "What are they filming, and why?"

"You have a match to play, I'll investigate," Grandpa responded. "I'll be back for the second half. Good luck, team!"

It was great to pull on my Throgmorton United shirt a short while later and forget all about computer mishaps for a while. As the drones seemed to have disappeared, I guessed Grandpa would be back in plenty of time to watch the match. My attention now turned to the pitch, and we were facing the Russian School Team, who looked formidable.

"Right, this team looks big and strong," said Mum as she gave us our final team talk. "Stand big and strong too, but use your speed."

With that, we entered the field of play and the whistle blew. Everyone was immediately on their game. Well, everyone except for Jemima and me. Big Keith put in a couple of crunching tackles. Viv was making great passes, and Raheem used all his speed to bamboozle the opposition. We were holding firm until Jemima and I got involved. I just couldn't seem to control the ball. My feet just didn't feel right, and every pass I made seemed to go astray. If I was playing badly, then Jemima, usually so reliable, was having a nightmare.

"I can't hold on to anything!" she complained as yet another ball slipped through her fingers. She was only being saved by Big Keith, who had discovered a great knack for knowing exactly when to stand on the goal line.

"Thanks, Keith," said a relieved Jemima as he saved another certain goal. The Russian team seemed to sense our discomfort and were now attacking in waves.

"Just make it to half-time," implored Mum.

"The data on these makes for bad reading for you two," warned Viv as she checked the footie headbands.

The half-time whistle finally blew, and we were delighted – and a little amazed – to come off the pitch at 0-0. Dad was convinced we were carrying knocks or had picked up some strange ailment. "Does this hurt? Is that sore?" he enquired as he desperately sought out potential injuries.

"I think my feet are itchy," I said.

Mum was staring at the analysis from our headbands.

"According to this data, there's something in your boots, Jez. Jemima, you need to look in your gloves."

"Blisters!" I sighed. The double training of foot-jitsu and regular football was catching up on me, and it was affecting my sister as well.

"I've got them on my hands, too," groaned Jemima. "Dad, it's your time to shine."

Dad got to work with a pile of plasters, bandages, creams and lotions, and soon we were all patched up. "Now, go play!" he mumbled before collapsing to the ground, exhausted.

The whistle went for the second half, and Jemima and I were like brand-new signings for our team. Suddenly, free of the irritating pain from the blisters, we could finally play properly. I was able to pass again and, with Jemima actually making saves, Big Keith could push up the pitch.

"Use some speed!" Mum shouted from the sidelines. It was great advice, but we had to bide our time. Midway through the second half, the Russian team started to tire. I didn't have to say anything as my body language made it clear it was time to pounce. Picking the ball up from Big Keith, I drove the team forward and was soon joined in attack by the whole team, barring Jemima.

"Big Keith!" I shouted as I lofted a ball over their defence to him. He curled a gorgeous shot straight into Viv's back! I think we had got a bit too keen!

Fortunately, the ball bounced kindly to Raheem whose practise of the steel ox super shot, obviously paid off – and he blasted past their diving keeper.

1-0!

The whistle sounded and we had won. After shaking hands with our opponents, we celebrated on the pitch, we celebrated on the coach, we celebrated in the hotel. It was only when we finally stopped celebrating that we noticed something was wrong.

SHOPPING CENTRE SEARCH

We were just about to sit down for dinner at the hotel when it struck me.

"Where's Grandpa?" I asked.

"We haven't seen him since he went after those drones," said Jemima.

Mum took us aside. "He wasn't at the game," she said. "We were all so concerned with the result that none of us even noticed!"

"I'm sure he'll show up," chirped Dad. "If he's not here in the morning, we'll get searching."

"There's no need to be worried," smiled Mum reassuringly. "After all, he is a grandmaster football ninja and, no matter what was happening with those drones, he will have encountered worse."

However, when the next day brought no sign of Grandpa, Mum and Dad decided it was time to start searching for him. Fortunately, it was a rest day so we didn't have training. While the rest of the team happily headed off to see jaguars and toucans at an eco-park, we stayed behind. From his makeshift mission control, Dad had spotted some interesting activity.

"Although all my computers have been affected by hackers, I have been able to keep some capacity going," he said as he activated a screen. "I picked up the drone

activity from yesterday. They seemed to be hovering around the downtown area. More specifically, the football pitch."

"What would they be looking for?" asked Jemima.

"I think if we can work that out, we will solve the case," said Dad. "What I also found is the area the drones came from. I think that's where we should start our search. Smedleys, we're going to the shops!"

Although we knew Grandpa could cope with just about any situation, Mum was now getting a little anxious.

"It's not like him not to get in touch after this length of time," declared Mum. "I'm not panicking, but we need to track him down. He may need our help."

We had soon crossed Rio by metro and found ourselves in a large shopping centre.

"So, the drones seem to have been coming from somewhere near here," observed Dad, looking at his hand-held monitor.

"Maybe Grandpa followed them back here?" wondered Mum.

It was hard to know where to start – we were surrounded by shops, restaurants and people enjoying an afternoon out. Using our ninja speed, Jemima and I quickly zipped between shops, and I even climbed up on to the roof to look down.

"A clothes shop, shoe shop, restaurants, Hi-Tech Toys ... Don't we have one of those at home?" I asked Jemima.

"They're a global chain," answered Jemima. "They're all over the world."

After an entire day in the shopping centre, the sun was about to set and it was getting dark. In fact, the shops were shutting and we had come up with nothing. We were about to depart when I noticed something glimmering in the sun – something I felt compelled to examine more closely.

"I recognise these – they're Grandpa's glasses!" I smiled, holding up a familiar pair of spectacles.

"So, he is close to here," beamed Mum, delighted to know Grandpa was somewhere in the vicinity.

Frustratingly, our search was about to come to an abrupt halt as it was closing time and the shopping centre staff began ushering us off the premises.

"We'll come back tomorrow," said Dad as we reluctantly left. "There's nothing in a shopping centre Grandmaster Smedley can't handle."

"Let's hope so. We will have to make it back here during the afternoon," said Mum. "Don't forget we have a match in the morning!"

Back at the hotel, the rest of the team had returned, and they were buzzing after their day at the eco-park.

"It was amazing!" trilled Raheem. "They had some wildlife in there that was actually faster than me!"

"I loved the huge trees and the multicoloured flowers," grinned Viv.

"Don't forget the creepy crawlies," said Big Keith. "They've got centipedes as thick as rope and spiders that could swallow a cat!"

"So, how was your day?" asked Mr Drabble.

"Oh, we went to a shopping centre," I said. "I know, I know – we travelled all the way to Brazil and went shopping. Not exactly a cultural outing!"

***

The next day dawned and there was still no sign of Grandpa. Although we were worried, Mum reassured us. "Never underestimate Grandpa – he's been in worse scrapes than this. We'll resume our search right after the match."

It was hard, but we were determined to focus on the quarter-final against the Australian School Rovers. Although none of the Smedleys really wanted to be involved, we all knew we couldn't let the team down – and the match proved to be a bit like our mood: a rather flat affair.

Dad spent most of the time on the sidelines looking at his computers and trying to find traces of Grandpa.

Meanwhile, Mum, who would usually have watched the game like a hawk – looking for tactical advantages, where we could play better, and weaknesses in the opposition – was busy working on a gadget for our potential mission.

It was hardly surprising that we were 1-0 down at half-time. Although Keith, Viv and Raheem had all worked really hard, Jemima and I were completely distracted.

"I know it's hard to focus on the football with your grandfather missing," said Mr Drabble, sympathetically. "But we must try to find a way to win this game."

"I'm sorry," I apologised.

"Me, too," mumbled Jemima.

Mum and Dad barely looked up, so who was going to coach the team? Who was going to give us the tactics to turn this around? Fortunately, we were saved by technology.

"The footie headbands' data," announced Viv. "Let's have a look. Right, it's clear that two players are not contributing to their usual level. Jez, Jemima – we need you to dig deep, just for the second half."

"Wait a second," said Dad looking at the screen in front of him. "The footie headbands are making a radical suggestion ..."

"It's crazy," chuckled Mum as she saw it too. "But it's got to be worth a try!"

When we saw the suggestion, we couldn't quite believe it – but we had no choice but to give it a go. The second half kicked off, and I was suddenly more focused than I had ever been. As for Jemima, the last time she had looked so committed was for her end-of-year exams. Following the footie headbands' advice, we had swapped positions!

I had never played a match in goal before, and it was completely different from my usual role. Outfield, I'm all action, always involved, always on the ball, but in goal it was the complete opposite. Nothing happened for ages, then suddenly everything happened at once! Jemima must have been having the same thoughts as me and she seemed to relish being super-busy.

"Great pass!" said Viv as Jemima rolled the ball into her path, but as I started to clap, the ball was stolen

off Raheem's toes by an Australian defender who then pinged the ball towards their striker.

"Jez!" shouted Jemima. Luckily, I was already off my line and intercepted the ball.

"Great save, Jez," said Keith. "Now, send it up the pitch!"

I took my time, then lobbed a beautiful ball right on to Jemima's head. She nodded the ball forward, towards Raheem, who planted a stunning, swerving shot past the opposition keeper's despairing dive.

1–1!

"Well done, guys," cheered Mum, pausing to look up from her gadget work to celebrate.

From that moment on, the opposition didn't stand a chance. I made a series of saves and Jemima provided the energy and power to the team that had been lacking in the first half. All that was needed was a winning goal, and when Raheem was brought down in the Australian box, there was only one penalty-taker.

"Go, Jemima!" cried Dad. "Just don't stub your toe!"

Fortunately, Jemima wasn't listening, because she stepped up and walloped a fantastic penalty straight past the Australian goalie.

2–1!

The full-time whistle blew and we were in the final, but as the rest of the team celebrated, we Smedleys knew we had a lot of work to do. As we tucked into our post-match meal in the shopping centre, little did we know that Grandpa was much, much closer than we thought!

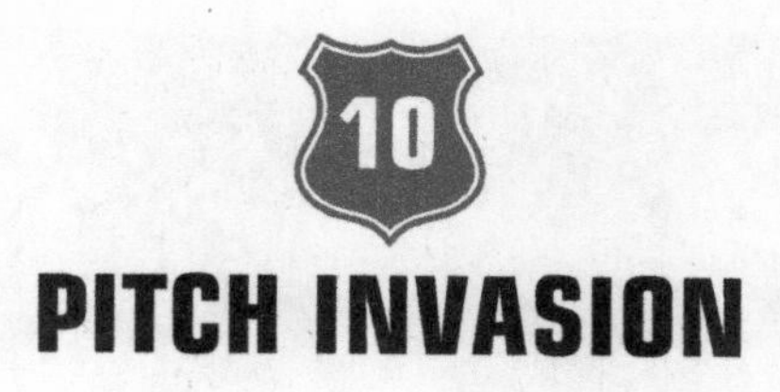

PITCH INVASION

"I need to thank you," leered Bad-Pixel as he paced around his underground lair. He was talking to Grandmaster Smedley, who glared at him defiantly despite being tied to a chair.

"If you hadn't been snooping around our drones, we might have missed it," added Lavinia Tech.

"Missed what?" snarled Grandmaster Smedley.

"The mother lode," chuckled Bad-Pixel. "All the phonium I need, right there, just waiting to be picked up."

"Phonium? What is that?" snapped Grandpa as he struggled against the ropes.

"You don't need to know," said Lavinia. "You'll discover soon enough. I really don't understand why we didn't think about accessing it via the football pitch. It's about the only part of Rio that isn't built on. Just wait until the digger gets to work there."

"Hey, you can't dig up that pitch!" shouted Grandmaster Smedley. "We need it for the Inter-School World Championship."

"I know," said Bad-Pixel matter-of-factly. "Which is why we are keeping you here so you don't report us."

"You can't simply destroy the pitch," ordered the Grandmaster. "The authorities will never allow it!"

"You are quite right," smiled the malevolent hi-tech expert, his grin as cheesy as the cheesiest cheese topping on an extra cheesy pizza. "Which is why I plan to liven things up a bit there. Create a favourable environment. Lavinia, is the Goliath 3000 ready to go?"

"I do believe it is," proclaimed Lavinia. "Watch with awe as you observe the power, the might, the fury of ... the Goliath 3000!"

She opened a tiny box and produced an underwhelming-looking computer the size of a matchbox.

"Just wait until we switch it on!" crowed Bad-Pixel with an unpleasant glint in his eye.

***

We woke up bright and early the next day. It was Saturday morning – the day before the final. The rest of the team would be conserving energy by lounging on the beach, but there was to be no rest for us – we had searching to do.

"There is no way we are playing the final without Grandpa being there," I stated as I put on my ninja kit.

"I don't believe his disappearance is a coincidence," said Dad. "I suspect someone is holding him – quite possibly the person behind the hi-tech attacks."

"We should find out as soon as we track Grandpa down," said Mum. "In the meantime, let's hope the cyber attacks don't escalate." Little did she know that a major escalation was exactly what was about to happen – and our investigation was about to be hugely diverted.

We were all set to head back to the shopping centre when, as we later discovered, across town Bad-Pixel activated the tiny computer. The full-blown cyber attack he had threatened was now unleashed. The effects were instantaneous and devastating – it wasn't just computers misbehaving, sat navs malfunctioning and hotel keys not working. This time, the impact was enormous. The first we became aware of it was when we left the hotel and attempted our second trip to the shopping centre.

"The metro has been cancelled," complained Dad when we reached the underground station.

"When's the next one?" asked Jemima.

"Er, never," said Dad, squinting at the electronic timetable, which flickered, then stopped working entirely. This was just the start of the problems. Before long, every corner of the city was impacted as lights in shops and cafes flickered on and off, and bank machines stopped giving out money. Traffic lights flashed randomly, causing cars and buses to swerve and collide, and planes were forced to make emergency landings.

"Good thing I've got my mobile set to a safe ninja-only network," said Dad. "This is an all-out cyber attack! We need to put the search for Grandpa on hold and stop this at once."

Looking up at the sky, which was now free of planes, a familiar object hovered into view.

"Look up there! It's our dear old friend, Mr Drone," said Mum. "We need to follow it on foot!"

"Don't go too fast because I don't want to pull a muscle, but I think we need to run," said Dad, stretching gingerly.

Jemima rolled her eyes. "Mum, you and Jez go ahead, we'll catch up."

Mum and I were soon charging across town, pounding past cars, over buses and around bewildered pedestrians. As we crossed the city, we could see people's phones randomly ringing, tablets smouldering and laptops fizzing. I was the fastest member of the family, but even I was only just managing to keep the drone in view. It was almost out of sight when it finally stopped moving. At first, I was just delighted not to have lost it, but then I realised exactly where it was hovering.

“It’s positioned over the football stadium!” I gasped.

The stadium seemed to be a hive of activity. Workmen were in the process of building a huge wall around it, and a colossal drill, standing almost as tall as the surrounding skyscrapers, was being assembled right in the middle of the pitch.

“Looks like the final has been cancelled,” said Dad as he approached the ticket office. “Even if there still was a pitch, all the ticketing computers are down.”

“What are they digging for? All I can see is red earth,” noticed Jemima.

“We need that drone,” said Dad. “If I could get my hands on it, I could probably hack it and find out where it’s come from.”

“Stand aside,” I said, picking up a stray football. “Time for some foot-jitsu …”

I took aim and, with an almost laser-guided level of accuracy, used the steel ox super shot to blast the ball – straight at Dad.

"Jez!" wailed my poor father, picking himself up. "I think I may have cracked a rib."

"Sorry, Dad! I'm still working on that move," I apologised. "Let me try a flying dragon header instead. Jemima – football, please."

Jemima tossed the ball in the air, and this time I hit it sweetly with a flying dragon header. The ball sizzled its way through the sky, smashing into the hovering drone, which glinted in the sunshine as it plummeted to earth.

"Bullseye!" grinned Mum as she retrieved the smouldering drone. "Now, let's get to work on this."

Dad was soon examining the circuits and inspecting the hardware powering the machine. "No clues here," he sighed. "Whoever is using this is smart and covered their tracks – there's nothing traceable on this device that I can detect."

It was then I noticed a small label stuck to the bottom of the drone. "Not that smart," I smiled. "Look at the label."

"I saw that," said Dad. "It's just the place that sold it. It doesn't tell us anything more than that."

"Really?" I chuckled. "'Hi-Tech Toys'. There's a branch in the shopping centre. I think we need to go there as soon as possible."

"Great ninja work, team" said Mum. "Right, Dad – have a quick stretch. It's going to be another long run!"

11 SHOPPING MAULED

"This is the worst cyber attack I have ever seen," huffed Dad as we vaulted a taxi whose faulty sat nav had sent it careering into a lamp post.

"I suspect whoever did this is creating a diversion to allow them to start mining the football pitch," said Mum.

"Well, hopefully all will become clear at Hi-Tech Toys," I gasped, not pausing for breath.

"Then we can find Grandpa!" added Jemima.

After jumping over a derailed train and skipping around an overturned fire engine, we finally made it back to the shopping centre. It was quiet … eerily quiet. You didn't have to be a football ninja to know this wasn't a good thing.

"I guess with all the chaos, not to mention the air-con being down, no one's in the mood to shop," whispered Dad as we approached the shopping centre.

"It's time for you two to go ahead," said Mum. "Four of us will be too conspicuous, but a couple of kids might be able to sneak past any security cameras."

"We'll set up a mini base here," whispered Dad as they hid behind an abandoned ice-cream concession. "And if we get peckish …" Unfortunately, melting ice-cream was oozing from underneath it.

"We have no idea what to expect, and it could be dangerous," warned Mum. "So wear these." She produced her latest gadget from her rucksack. "Hover shin pads. Only deploy them if you absolutely have to. I think you will find them quite 'uplifting'."

With Mum's newest gadget strapped around our shins, we noticed a flash of colour in the distance. If we hadn't been looking out for our villain, we might have thought it was an Amazonian parrot or a clown. Fortunately, Jemima identified it right away.

"That man who's going into the tech toyshop," she whispered. "We've seen him before ..."

"In the airport shop," I responded.

"This has got to be it," said Jemima. "Let's go!"

As we started our slow, low-profile approach to Hi-Tech Toys International, the numerous security cameras made us both aware it was not going to be easy. We used ninja stealth to approach the store unseen. We hid in pot plants, somersaulted from one hiding point to the next and, finally, we shimmied up the side of a burger restaurant. Although a little precarious, we were now perched with the perfect vantage point to look down at the shop entrance below.

"Check out that skylight," I said, pointing out a slightly tilted glass opening in the roof. "I assume that's where the drones come in and out from."

"Well spotted," said Jemima. "Look, the main door is open."

"This guy is so confident we won't find him that he left the door open," I smiled. "Well, it's time for a nasty ninja surprise!"

We quietly descended the drainpipe from the burger restaurant roof and, keeping as low as possible, carefully entered the toyshop. Like the rest of the shopping centre, the place was not only deserted, but spookily quiet.

"No sign of anyone in a bright shirt," I whispered. "Or Grandpa."

"He can't have just disappeared," responded Jemima. "There must be another room or antechamber."

Staying low and moving as quietly as we could, we ventured deeper into the shop. Then I spotted a further door and, beyond it, a staircase.

"This must be it," I said urgently as we started to descend the stairs. "Our man hasn't made any effort to hide at all."

I spoke too soon. On the third step, we heard a distinctive clicking sound. Immediately, the staircase turned into a steep, slippery ramp. We were now sliding down, down, down ... into a trap!

"Why, hello!" It was the man in the Hawaiian shirt. "I've been expecting you. In fact, you may have wondered why it was so easy to find me. It's almost as if I left you a trail of clues ..."

I thought back to Grandpa's discarded glasses, the label on the drone and the open doors ... so it had all been a trap.

"You're right where I want you. I don't need any football ninjas getting in the way when I complete my operation."

"What operation? Who are you?" I snapped.

"Oh, I'm sorry, how rude of me. Let me introduce myself: I am Darren Bad-Pixel and this is my colleague, Lavinia Tech. You'll find out all about my operation soon enough."

"Have you got Grandpa?" hissed Jemima.

"And what are you plotting?" I added.

"Oh, your beloved grandpa! He is alive and well," gloated Bad-Pixel. "You'll be joining him right away."

"We need to go, Mr Bad-Pixel," interrupted Lavinia. "The final part of the plan requires our attention."

With that, we were bundled through a second door that slammed shut and locked behind us.

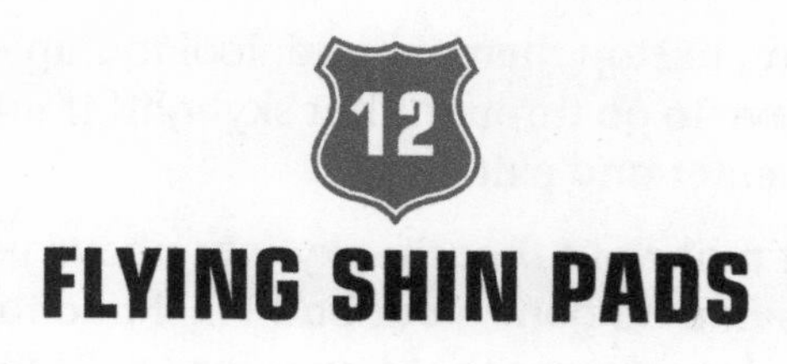

FLYING SHIN PADS

Our initial disappointment at being so gullible soon evaporated when we saw who else was with us. In the corner of the dank storeroom, among buckets and mops and piles of junk, was someone we were incredibly happy to see.

"Grandpa!" we shouted, delighted to be reunited with our no-longer-long-lost relative.

"I wish I could say it was great to see you, but this means his trap worked. On all of us ..." sighed Grandpa, who seemed simultaneously pleased and annoyed to see us.

That was when we noticed Mum and Dad sitting behind a pile of cardboard boxes.

"We were caught by a couple of his motley crew as soon as you set off," said Mum.

"I'm starting to feel seriously claustrophobic," complained Dad. "This place is overcrowded, damp and probably plagued by dangerous spiders, not to mention—"

"Well, he has to be brought to justice," interrupted Grandpa. "I've used my super-strong ninja hearing to listen in on them, and I know exactly what their plan is."

Grandpa explained their nasty plot to shut the city down and use the chaos to mine all the phonium at the football stadium, which included leaving the pitch permanently unplayable.

"We're going to stop them," I said, looking upwards. "We're going to have to go through that skylight! It must be where the drones enter and exit."

I could just make out that the skylight above us was ajar. The drones had all gone – but Bad-Pixel had forgotten to shut it! The trouble was that it was far too high to get out of, unless …

"Gadget time!" declared Mum. "I can't wait to see my hover shin pads in action. Press the button to fire up the mini rockets!"

We reached down to our socks, each pressed the button on this latest gadget and, at once, we started to rise as the mini rockets on the sides of the shin pads fired into action.

"Wow! These are amazing!" I shouted.

"Although they are a bit tricky to steer," said Jemima as she narrowly missed me.

The shin pads were awkward to manoeuvre at first but, after bumping our heads on the walls a couple of times, we started to get the hang of them.

"Be careful out there!" warned Mum as we took off and hovered towards the open skylight above.

"They said they were heading to Sugarloaf Mountain," shouted Grandpa as we reached our improvised exit. "You should go there!"

I nudged the skylight fully open – and we were out!

"This is the way to travel!" I said to Jemima as we glided above the city.

"Look at the turmoil in the streets," observed Jemima. We could make out stalled traffic and irate inhabitants milling around beneath us. Soon, we were swooping towards Sugarloaf Mountain, the amazing peak of land that looms over Rio. That's when we spotted our villain and his sidekick a little way ahead of us.

"Look! They're in that drone pod!" I called to Jemima. "Let's keep our distance and pounce when we see where they land."

Fortunately, our hover shin pads were quiet, and Bad-Pixel and Tech seemed completely oblivious that we were shadowing them.

"Unbelievable! They seem to have set up some sort of mission control up here," I pointed out as we watched them landing their drone at the very top of the mountain. "It's time to close them down for good."

Jemima and I touched down in an area of shrubs a discreet distance away, but our element of surprise was all too short-lived. A mini drone had spotted us!

"I've been watching you ever since you left the shop," smirked Bad-Pixel. "That drone followed you all the way from the shopping centre. I beamed it all to my trusty wrist screen. So, what are those things on your legs? Some sort of flying shin pads? We'll need to sell those in my shops when I am in control of all the technology in the world!"

"First, we'll send you right back to where you came from!" cackled Lavinia. She pressed a button, and we were suddenly surrounded by buzzing drones.

“Time for some foot-jitsu!” I cried as Jemima and I used our lightning leopard turbo dribble to zip past the cordon of drones.

“Now for some iron tiger tackles – let’s make them flying iron tiger tackles!” I winked at Jemima. Powering up the mini rockets on my hover shin pads, I flew at the drones feet first, smashing several to the ground with my flying tackle.

“Leave some for me, Jez!” cried Jemima as she, too, fizzed through the air and took out more of the hovering menaces.

With most of the mini drones downed, we could now turn our attention to Bad-Pixel and his mission control zone. We could clearly see him furiously pressing buttons on a large computer, but getting to him would be hard, really hard.

“He’s surrounded by drones,” I said.

"They're hovering all round him, protecting his computer," said Jemima.

There's one last thing we could try, I thought to myself. I'd noticed an old, discarded football in the undergrowth. It was slightly deflated but still functional. "Jemima, lob that ball up to me," I hissed urgently.

"Really, you're playing football?!" scoffed Bad-Pixel. "Well, you might as well play here. Your pitch is about to disappear – just as soon as I press this button and give the command to power up the drills and commence the deep excavation."

That was it – there was no way we were going to allow that to happen.

"Now!" I shouted, and Jemima lobbed me the ball. For a second, time stood still. All my foot-jitsu training flashed before my eyes as I jumped and …

"STEEL OX SUPER SHOT!" I cried. With that, I smashed the ball with such force that it became a blur as it bulldozed its way through the drones before pulverising Bad-Pixel's computer. There was a loud fizz, a flash of sparks and an even louder bang. Then silence.

"Great job, Jez!" smiled Jemima as a police helicopter now hovered into view. "Looks like it's 'game over' for Bad-Pixel."

"Great job, sis!" I replied. "Now we've got a match to play!"

THE FINAL FINAL

Back at the hotel, everything had returned to normal. The rest of the team were delighted to hear the pitch was saved, ticket sales had resumed, and the match was back on. Mr Drabble had heard from the tournament organiser that once the giant drill had been removed, we could play. Fortunately, the digging had stopped just before permanent damage was done to the pitch.

This was excellent news, but I had no sooner got my kit on than I realised we had forgotten something rather important: Mum, Dad and Grandpa! Jemima and I were about to set off back to the shopping centre when there was a knock at the door.

"Well done, team!" beamed Grandpa. With him were Mum and Dad. "You saved the day!"

"You got out!" I gasped.

"You don't lose your foot-jitsu skills when you get older," chuckled Mum. "After you left, we got to work!"

"I dusted off one of my favourite moves," said Grandpa. "The jaguar claw grip. We all used it to clamber our way out. Even Dad."

"Did you see how high that wall was?" whimpered Dad, who still looked a little shaken up. "I think I broke a fingernail."

"It's a great technique, but it is slow and painful,"

interrupted Mum. "Good thing you had the hover shin pads or we'd have been too late. We called the police as soon as we could."

We heard a loud shout from outside. It was Mr Drabble.

"Come on, Smedleys. The bus is waiting!"

***

As we drove to the stadium, we could see the city getting back to normal. Cars were driving around, trams were picking up passengers, and planes were taking off and landing again. When we reached the arena, we could see it had been reopened. The great drilling rig had been dismantled and was being driven out on huge trailers.

"To think this pitch might have been dug up forever just so a greedy villain could make cheap tech," I said to Jemima as we admired our handiwork.

"Look at the mayhem he caused with just one cyber attack," added Jemima. "With his own phones, tablets and computers, he would have taken over the world."

Now, although the thought of Bad-Pixel controlling the world's technology was scary, we soon spotted an even scarier challenge – our next opponents: the Brazilian Soccer Kings. Mum and Dad were about to give us our team talk when Viv made a big decision.

"After all that's happened, I think we should play this match without technology," she said. "Let's hand in our footie headbands."

Reluctantly at first, we handed the headbands to Dad.

"I think it's the right call," Mum reassured us. "Football is about teamwork, effort and artistry. Technology does play a role but, for today, I agree we should go back to basics."

"I think Mrs Norbertson will be really impressed with your gadget anyway, Viv," said Jemima. This was high praise since she was the expert at impressing teachers!

"Right," said Mum. "Time to evaluate our opponents' weaknesses, which won't take long – they don't have any."

"They're skilful, fast, powerful and smart," added Mr Drabble unhelpfully.

"But so are we," said Mum. "So, let's go out there and give it our best shot!"

We jogged out on to the pitch and took our positions. The whistle blew, and we were soon feeling overwhelmed – the Brazilian team's familiar yellow shirts seemed to be everywhere. We needed to catch up with the pace of the game – and fast!

"They're behind us, in front of us and next to us at the same time," complained Big Keith who, as the team's defender, had never been worked so hard. "It's devastating and brilliant!"

Now, when you come up against such illustrious and skilled opposition, you can go one of two ways: you rise to the challenge, or you raise your hands and admit defeat. When they scored their first goal after a piece of outrageous skill from their striker, it was time to rise to the challenge.

0-1

We dug really deep and put a bit more energy into every tackle, save and shot. We might not have turned the Brazilian tide, but at least we held it back until the half-time whistle.

With no technology to tell us about our number of tackles, how hard we were shooting and whether or not we'd covered enough ground, it was refreshing to have a good, old-fashioned team talk from Mum.

"We knew this team would be good," she started, "so it's time for each of us to really think about how much we are giving, and to give a bit more. It's the last game of the tournament, so don't hold back – it's now or never!"

"That's the spirit," added Mr Drabble. "There is no shame in losing as long as we've tried our best!"

We all regained our breath, drank lots of water and ate some half-time papayas. I could sense a new streak of determination running through the team. Fortunately, the Brazilian team were showboating outrageously in the second half – juggling the ball, attempting flamboyant overhead kicks and trying to dribble the

length of the pitch. If we hadn't been playing, this would have been great to watch, but being on the receiving end just made us more determined.

Jemima made a series of great saves and sent the ball to Big Keith, who barrelled forward sending a Brazilian attacker flying. He bundled the ball to Viv, who quickly slipped it in my direction. I then rode out a couple of challenging tackles before shifting the ball to Raheem.

"Banana kick!" Mum implored at the top of her voice.

Raheem hit a perfect bending shot that curled and dipped towards the top corner of the goal. At the very last second, their keeper, who had largely been a spectator up to then, arched his back, and his fingertips tipped the ball on to the cross bar. Noooo! Our best chance had narrowly failed to go in, or had it? Time seemed to stand still as the ball rebounded off the bar and bounced back into play, towards me. I had a chance to shoot, but I was far out and most of the Brazilian team seemed to be standing between me and the goal. It was then I made my decision ...

"STEEL OX SUPER SHOT!" I cried, before slamming the ball with all the power I had used on Bad-Pixel.

The Brazilian defenders stood still, their mouths agape as the ball shot past them and the goalie's dive.

1-1!

Game on! Well, it was for about five minutes, because then something strange started happening on the pitch. Raheem noticed it first when, for no reason, he fell over.

"Hey, that bit of ground moved," claimed our super-fast star striker.

“The ground can’t move,” scoffed Big Keith, seconds before he, too, went flying.

“There’s something happening under the pitch,” I declared, my ninja senses tingling.

It was then that I noticed Jemima starting to rise into the air, not because of her hover shin pads but because the ground under her was lifting up.

“It’s some sort of vehicle!” shouted Mum, spotting the cause of this frightening pitch invasion. Sure enough, a vehicle shaped like a tank, but with an immense drill at the front, emerged from under the ground. At the wheel was our old foe.

“Bad-Pixel!” bellowed Jemima as she scrambled to safety.

“Did you really think the police could hold me!” he scoffed. “I hacked the police station security system in ten minutes. Now it’s time to fill this vehicle with phonium, and then I’ll be on my way.”

“Never!” shouted Grandpa from the stands. Opening a storage cabinet beside the pitch, he began kicking and heading footballs towards us. “Jez, Jemima! Get to it!”

Jemima and I jumped into action. We were both smashing steel ox super shots at the digger, but they were having no effect. We needed more.

“I’ll help!” said Raheem, and he, too, took a shot at the digger.

“And us!” said Viv and Big Keith.

With the whole team involved, Bad-Pixel looked nervous for the first time. That look turned to abject fear when every member of the Brazilian Soccer Kings also got involved! Soon, the digger was being bombarded with footballs from every angle, and Bad-Pixel was losing control.

“Here goes!” I shouted as I summoned the energy for a final dose of foot-jitsu. I took aim and blasted a steel ox super shot right at the cockpit of Bad-Pixel’s vehicle. The glass shattered and the digger wobbled, then toppled on to its side. Like a tortoise on its back, the vehicle could no longer move.

"We've done it!" we all cheered.

We were all keen to carry on with the game, but the pitch was so badly damaged it had been rendered unplayable. After some discussions with the tournament organiser, it was decided that both teams would share the trophy!

Everyone was delighted as we stepped on to the podium with the Brazilian team to receive our medals. Cheers rang across the stadium as Mum and Dad performed an impromptu samba and Mr Drabble blew his whistle with delight. We were even invited to share a special celebratory dinner with the opposing team! But before we could leave the pitch, Grandpa emerged from the crowd.

"Congratulations, Jez and Jemima. In recognition of all your amazing foot-jitsu skills, I award you BOTH the

black belt in foot-jitsu! We couldn't have defeated Bad-Pixel without your teammates from Throgmorton United and, of course, the Brazilian Soccer Kings," he added. "So everyone gets a special one-off honorary orange belt!

***

The following day, exhausted but content, I slumped into my airline seat for the long flight home. "Well, it's been some journey," I sighed.

"Yes, Throgmorton United have come a long way from playing local games," smiled Mum.

"All the while fighting crime and defeating super-villains with foot-jitsu," added Dad.

"When we started out, we were only planning to play a few football games, but we ended up saving the world!" I chuckled.

"Jemima, what do you think?" asked Mum. There was no response. Jemima was already doing her homework, which reminded me about the project for Mrs Norbertson. I needed to speak urgently with Viv and make sure the footie headbands are ready to show. When I joined the rest of the team at the back of the plane, they were just about to be addressed by Mr Drabble.

"Fear not, team! I have already put my feelers out for our next football tournament," said our head teacher. "Training starts tomorrow ..."

We all groaned, but I was already excited about our next match and our next ninja mission. In fact, I reminded myself to ask Grandpa to teach me that jaguar claw grip move as soon as we got back!

Now answer the questions ...

1 Look back at the Contents page. Which two chapter titles play with words to make their meaning ambiguous?

2 Give the meaning of the word 'monologue' (page 15).

3 What is the name of Darren Bad-Pixel's chain of shops?

4 Why does Bad-Pixel use the expression 'a carnival of nastiness' when he talks about going to Rio?

5 Why was Grandpa 'simultaneously pleased and annoyed' to be reunited with Jez and Jemima in Chapter 12?

6 On how many occasions does Bad-Pixel lay a trap for the Smedleys? Give examples from the text to support your answer.

7 Do you think the rest of Jez and Jemima's team have any idea that the Smedleys are crime-stopping football ninjas? Does it make any difference to how they work as a team?

8 How does this story compare to a) other stories in the Jez Smedley series; b) any other football-themed books you have read; c) any spy thrillers that you might be familiar with.